Inspired by **A. A.**

Winnie-the-Pooh
Tells Time

With Decorations by

ERNEST H. SHEPARD

Dutton Children's Books

NEW YORK

Illustrations by E. H. Shepard hand-colored by Eleanor Kwei
Typography by Richard Amari
Published in the United States by Dutton Children's Books,
a division of Penguin Books USA Inc.
375 Hudson Street, New York, New York 10014
Manufactured in China
First Edition
ISBN 0-525-45535-3

7:00 a.m.

It's seven o'clock.

Good morning, Pooh.

8:00 a.m.

It's **eight** o'clock.

Time for breakfast.

10:00 a.m.

It's **ten** o'clock.

Pooh does his
exercises.

11:00 a.m.

It's **eleven** o'clock.

Time for a little
smackerel of
something.

12:00 p.m.

It's **twelve** o'clock.

Lunchtime.

1:00 p.m.

It's **one** o'clock.

Pooh sings a
new song.

2:00 p.m.

It's two o'clock.

Pooh wants
another smackerel.

3:00 p.m.

It's three o'clock.

Pooh

 practices

jumping.

4:00 p.m.

It's **four** o'clock.

Pooh and Piglet go
to Owl's house for
a Proper Tea.

5:00 p.m.

It's **five** o'clock.

Time for a game of
Poohsticks.

6:00 p.m.

It's six o'clock.

Dinnertime.

8:00 p.m.

It's **eight** o'clock.

Good night, Pooh.